Foul Play

Written by
Karen King

Published by Hopscotch Educational Publishing Ltd,
29 Waterloo Place, Leamington Spa CV32 5LA
Tel: 01926 744227

© 2001 Hopscotch Educational Publishing

Written by Karen King
Series design by Blade Communications
Illustrated by Trevor Parkin
Printed by Clintplan, Southam

Karen King hereby asserts her moral right to be identified
as the author of this work in accordance with the
Copyright, Designs and Patents Act, 1988.

ISBN 1-902239-91-1

Chapter One

It was the start of the football season and Wednesday, after school, meant football practice for the Little Mulberry Football Club – otherwise known as the Red Berries.

As soon as the players arrived at the sports hut they crowded around the notice board, eager to find out if they'd been picked for the team.

The Red Berries were competing in the Under 11's Junior League and everyone wanted a part of the action.

Matt Blubb scanned the list of names and heaved a sigh of relief. He was in! Then he did a double-take. He was not only in – he was captain!

But his twin sister Kirsty wasn't so lucky. She was just a substitute.

Kirsty was even more annoyed when she saw that Dozy Dobbs was in the team. And playing as a striker – her usual position!

Matt felt sorry for his sister. He knew how he'd have felt if he hadn't made the team. Especially if he'd been dropped for someone who had only moved into the town a few weeks ago.

He could see why Rick, the coach, had chosen Tommy though. Kirsty was a mean player for a girl. But Tommy Dobbs was something else. He might look a bit dozy but when he got hold of that ball his feet practically grew wings. And he was brilliant at scoring goals.

Paul, Rosie, Iqbal and Tommy were also in the team.

"Okay everyone, you've seen what positions you're playing. Now get changed and let's get on that pitch!" Rick Jarvis shouted, coming out of the changing rooms.

On the pitch, Matt threw himself into the game, determined, to prove he was good enough to be captain.

"Well played team," Rick told everyone after the training session. "Carry on like that and we just might win the league."

Chapter Two

As Matt was about to leave Rick clapped him on the shoulder. "I'd like to have a word with you about your sister, Matt."

"It's tough for Kirsty at the moment, Matt," said Rick. "She's a good player and I know she's disappointed about not being in the team but unfortunately I can't include everyone. So give her a bit of support, eh?"

Kirsty was waiting for him.
"Telling you what a
brilliant captain you'd
make, was he?"

YEAH, RIGHT, THAT'S WHY I'M NOT IN THE TEAM

ACTUALLY, RICK WAS SAYING WHAT A GOOD PLAYER YOU ARE

"Come on, Kirst, everyone
can't be in the team!"
Matt told her.

Kirsty shrugged. "I guess I'll just
have to hope someone gets
dropped from the team, then I
can prove just how good I am."

The Red Berries' first match was against the Shafton Strikers, a team with a really tough reputation.

Determined to show Rick that he was reliable, Matt arrived bright and early for football practice on Sunday morning, only to find the coach muttering crossly as he fumbled with the lock.

Finally, after twenty minutes of messing with the lock, by which time all the other members of the team had arrived and were grumbling loudly, Rick gave up.

Thankfully, the lock had been unblocked by Wednesday. The Red Berries quickly changed into their kit, eager to get out onto the pitch. But this time they found, to their dismay, that the football was missing.

They looked all over the changing rooms but there was no sign of it.

So Rick had to go home and get
the spare ball. Half of the practice
session was over
by the time
he returned.

OK EVERYONE, LET'S GET OUT ONTO THE PITCH.

As he led the team on to the pitch Matt couldn't help thinking they were jinxed. First they're locked out, then the football goes missing. Talk about bad luck!

"Forget about it," he told himself sternly as he kicked the ball, sending it upfield. "Concentrate on playing football!"

Rosie Bray, the midfielder, intercepted the ball and delivered it to Tommy Dobbs who raced up to the goal with it, whooshed it past Peter O'Reilly's outstretched hands and nestled it in the far left corner of the net.

"Wicked!" Matt thought in admiration. With Dozy Dobbs in the team they had a good chance of beating the Shafton Strikers.

"Make sure you're all here bright and early on Sunday morning," Rick told everyone in the changing room afterwards. "I want to try out some new tactics."

The sun was shining brightly on Sunday morning as Matt and Kirsty hurried to the sports hut.

To Matt's relief, Kirsty had stopped sulking about only being a sub and was practising like mad, hoping one of the other players would twist an ankle or catch measles so she could play instead.

Some of the others were already in the changing room when Matt got there. He sat down beside them and unzipped his kit bag.

"Only another week until the match," Paul said as he pulled on his jersey. "I can't wait to ... hey what's happened to my jumper?"

His usually long jumper now ended just above his waist whilst the sleeves reached just below his elbows.

"Ha, ha! Look's like you're wearing your kid brother's jumper!" laughed Matt, shoving his feet into his football boots.

Only they weren't his boots. They
were someone else's
and they were so
big he almost
stepped out of
them as he
walked.

Around him, the other players
were all moaning about their kit.

Peter's jumper was so long you couldn't see his shorts and the sleeves were flapping over his hands.

Rosie couldn't get her boots on and Iqbal's shorts were so baggy he had to clutch them tight to stop them falling around his ankles!

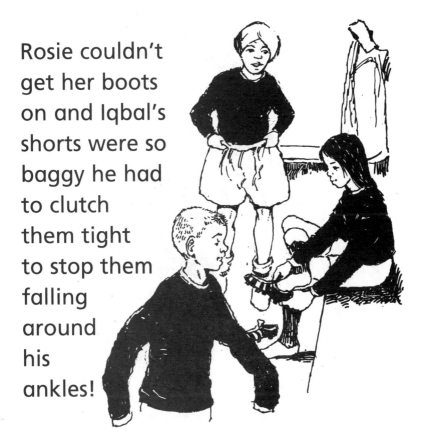

Matt groaned, by the time they'd sorted out everyone's kit they would hardly have any time to practise again.

Then an awful thought struck him. Their kit couldn't have got mixed up by accident. Someone had done it deliberately.

The same person had probably blocked up the lock and hidden the ball too. Someone was trying to make sure they didn't have much time to practise for their match next week.

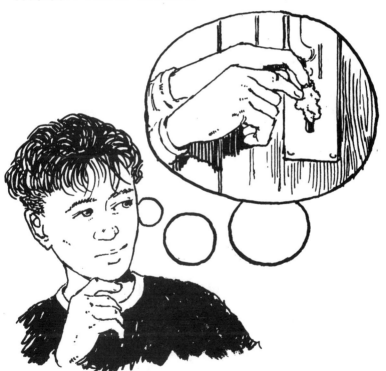

Someone wanted to make sure they lost the match!

Chapter Three

Matt confided his fears to Kirsty on the way home.

Matt frowned. "I'm not sure," he said. "But there's one thing I am sure of – all these things that keep going wrong aren't accidents. Someone's out to get us."

"Don't be daft," Kirsty scoffed. "How could anyone sneak in the sports hut and hide the ball or mix up the football kit – the door's always locked."

I'VE JUST GOT TO FIND OUT WHO'S DOING THIS

"I don't know. But I'm going to make sure nothing else happens," Matt said determinedly. "This is the first time I've ever been captain, and I want to win this match!"

Matt left early for football practice on Wednesday evening. He figured that whoever was playing dirty tricks on them had to arrive at the sports hut before everyone else, so he wanted to lie in wait for the culprit.

But no one turned up. And the training session passed without incident.

Maybe Kirsty was right, Matt thought. Maybe it was all just a coincidence. He'd better stop worrying and concentrate on winning the game on Saturday instead.

On Saturday morning, everyone arrived bright and early at the sports hut. The match was being held at the Little Mulberry Sports Ground so at least they were on home territory.

The Shafton Strikers' team had already arrived and were huddled in a corner of the pitch, deep in conversation with their coach.

THEY LOOK A MEAN BUNCH!

YEAH I BET THEY PLAY MEAN, TOO!

When they walked into the changing room, they found Rosie in a state of panic.

Frog was their lucky mascot. He usually sat on the top of the cupboard in the changing rooms. But for a match he was taken down, dusted and placed on the seat next to the coach.

The Red Berries had never played a game without Frog watching over them.

Matt knew with a sickening certainty that Frog's disappearance wasn't accidental.

SOMEONE'S STOLEN HIM. THEY'RE HOPING THAT WE'LL BE TOO UPSET ABOUT LOSING OUR LUCKY MASCOT TO PLAY PROPERLY

Worse was to come. When they changed into their football kit they discovered that the laces were missing out of all the football boots.

Chapter Four

Everyone stared at him.

"Think about it," said Matt. "We've never had so much stuff go wrong. Someone's doing it on purpose and who except the Shafton Strikers would want to mess up our chance of winning the game?"

For a moment there was dead silence as Rick considered this remark.

MATT COULD BE RIGHT. SO LET'S MAKE SURE THEY DON'T SUCCEED. GET ONTO THAT PITCH AND PLAY TO WIN!

Paul dashed out to ask his dad to buy more laces for everyone. Mr Garcia returned with them just in time for the match to start. So the Red Berries quickly laced up their boots and raced onto the pitch.

But they were all too flustered and upset about the loss of their mascot to play their best. And Matt's suspicions had been right. The Shafton Strikers did play dirty.

OWWW!

Even Tommy Dobbs wasn't on his usual good form.

With only ten minutes to go before half-time the Shafton Strikers were leading 2–0.

Matt groaned. At this rate they were going to lose the game. And whoever was trying to sabotage their chances was probably planning another surprise to greet them at half time, just to make sure they didn't play well in the second half. He had to get to the changing rooms quickly to try and catch them in the act. And there was only one way to do it!

AARGH! I'VE GOT CRAMP

Rick came running over to investigate.

He looked around. There was no sign of Kirsty. "Where is that girl?"

That's just like Kirsty, Matt thought as he hobbled to the changing rooms, she was dying to play in the team and as soon as she gets a chance she disappears.

Where had she gone to? He pushed open the door and walked into the sports hut, planning to hide so he could catch the Shafton saboteur red-handed. Instead he came face to face with his sister.

Chapter Five

OF COURSE IT'S NOT ME, STUPID! WHY WOULD I WANT YOU TO LOSE? I'M ON THE SAME TEAM, REMEMBER?

"So you can get a chance to play next time, that's why!" Matt snapped. "Which is what you're supposed to be doing right now. Taking my place until half time."

"Why? What's up with you?" Kirsty eyed him suspiciously.

"I pretended I had cramp so I could get sent off and try to catch whoever was playing all those sneaky tricks on us." He glared furiously as his sister. "Good job I did, too? What were you planning this time?"

"That's right," retorted Kirsty. "I saw him sneaking out of the hut this morning, looking really guilty. And he's been playing awful, like he's trying to give the game away. So I thought I'd check out his bag, see if he was the one behind all the tricks."

AND I WAS RIGHT!

Matt stared at her. Tommy Dobbs was their star player. Why would he want them to lose the game?

BUT WHY WOULD TOMMY DO THIS TO US?

But he knew his sister. She was a pain sometimes but she wasn't a sneak or a liar. And now he thought about it, it seemed like Tommy had deliberately missed a couple of shots at goal.

Matt and Kirsty exchanged glances. Then Kirsty turned around and looked Tommy straight in the face.

Everyone stared at Tommy.
He went red and looked down
at his feet.

"Well, Tommy, we're waiting for an explanation." Rick had his arms folded across his chest and a stern expression on his face.

Beefy Brown was the Shafton Strikers' captain. A big, hefty lad with a nasty temper.

"Then why didn't you come and tell me?" Rick asked. "You know that I won't stand for any bullying."

Matt looked at Tommy. He had gone white. Whatever Beefy Brown had threatened to do to him, it had really scared him.

"You should have told us, Tommy. We'd all stick by you. There's no way we'd let that creep bash you," Matt said.

Tommy looked as if he was about to cry. "You don't understand, he didn't threaten to hit me …"

He sat down, really slow like he felt all heavy.

HE SAID HE'D TELL YOU ABOUT MY DAD. HE ISN'T WORKING AWAY LIKE I TOLD EVERYONE. HE'S IN PRISON.

Chapter Six

SO WHAT? THAT'S NOT YOUR FAULT

"I know, but it's hard making friends when you're new," Tommy said quietly. "I thought you lot wouldn't want to know me if you found out about my dad."

"That's rubbish. We don't care what your dad's done!" Matt told him.

The others nodded in agreement. Rick looked stern. "I'll have a word with that young man's coach after the game. But right now we'd better get back on the pitch. It's almost time for the second half to start."

He turned to Matt, a twinkle in his eye. "I gather your leg is better now, Matt?"

"Er, yes it's fine," Matt nodded.

Tommy stood up.

There was silence for a minute.
Matt looked at Kirsty. He knew
how much she wanted to play but
he had to speak up.

"I think Tommy should play, otherwise it looks like we're giving into the bully Beefy Brown," he said.

Kirsty stared at him. Then she nodded.

"Okay," Rick agreed. "Tommy, you're in. Now everyone get onto the pitch and show those Shafton Strikers just what we're made of!" So they did!

GOAL!!!!!!

Tommy scored another goal. The score was even. But that wasn't good enough for Matt. He wanted to beat the Shafton Strikers. He wanted to show Beefy Brown that he couldn't bully people and get away with it.

Beefy Brown had the ball but Rosie neatly got it off him and sent it soaring upfield to Matt, who jumped up and headed it into the goal.

YES!

The Red Berries' supporters were
screaming so loud Matt barely
heard the final
whistle blow.

The game was over. They'd won.

Chapter Seven

Beefy Brown was furious.
He marched off the pitch, straight
over to Tommy Dobbs.

Matt and the others
gathered around Tommy.

"Brown, I want a word with you!" It was the Shafton coach, and he looked really annoyed. Behind him Rick grinned and put his thumb up. He'd obviously told the coach all about Beefy's bullying.

"I don't reckon you'll have any more trouble with Beefy," Matt told Tommy as the Shafton coach led off a sheepish-looking Beefy Brown.

"Thanks to you lot," Tommy replied. "I'm really sorry about everything. I wish I'd told you all about Beefy sooner."

DON'T WORRY ABOUT IT. WE WON AND THAT'S ALL THAT MATTERS

Laughing, the Red Berries headed off happily to change. Their first match of the season had been a brilliant success!

The Red Berries were still on a high when they piled into the sports hut for the following Wednesday's training session.

Everyone crowded around the notice board eager to see who'd been picked for the team for the next match.

Matt was pleased to see that he was captain again.

Tommy Dobbs was in too.

And to her delight, so was Kirsty.

BRILL! I'M IN THE TEAM

NICE ONE!